DATE DUE			
	4A		
	102		
	10		
	OCT 1 8 2004		
	OCT 0 3 2005		

SMALL WOLF

Story by Nathaniel Benchley

Pictures by Joan Sandin

HarperCollins*Publishers*

Small Wolf
Text copyright © 1972 by Nathaniel Benchley
Illustrations copyright © 1972, 1994 by Joan Sandin
Printed in the U.S.A.   All rights reserved.

Library of Congress Cataloging-in-Publication Data
Benchley, Nathaniel, date
   Small Wolf / story by Nathaniel Benchley ; pictures by Joan Sandin.
      p.   cm. — (An I can read book)
   Summary: A young Native American boy sets out to hunt on Manhattan
Island and discovers some strange people with very different ideas about land.
   ISBN 0-06-020491-5. — ISBN 0-06-020492-3 (lib. bdg.)
   1. Indians of North America—Juvenile fiction.   [1. Indians of North
America—Fiction.]   I. Sandin, Joan, ill.   II. Title.   III. Series.
PZ7.B4312Sm   1994   93-26717
[E]—dc20   CIP
                                                                          AC

Typography by Al Cetta
1   2   3   4   5   6   7   8   9   10
❖
Newly Illustrated Edition

SMALL WOLF

Small Wolf lived with his family

in a village

on the banks of a river.

His mother planted corn
and did the cooking,
and his father did the hunting.

6

His father hunted deer and bears

and smaller things to eat.

What they didn't eat

they made into clothes.

But Small Wolf

was too small to go hunting.

All he could do

was fish from his canoe.

He caught fish

with a hook made of bone.

And he caught fish
with a net of woven string.
He also caught eels
and dug for clams and oysters.
It was a good life,
and he liked fishing.

But after a while

he tired of catching fish.

He wanted to hunt for bigger things.

He asked his father

to let him try.

"After all," he said,

"what can I lose?

An arrow or two,

and that's all."

"All right," his father said.

"There is good hunting

on the Island of Hills, downriver.

Take your canoe,

and spend a night

and a day there,

and see what luck you have."

"Ya-hoo!" cried Small Wolf.

He got in his canoe

and went to Manhattan,

the Island of Hills.

"If I hunt well here," he thought,

"and shoot a lot of deer and bears

and foxes and wolves

and moose and eagles

and weasels and otters

and skunks and wildcats,

then I will be a man like my father.

"I'll be able to wear
feathers in my hair
and colors on my face."

He did not know

that to be a man was more

than just shooting things.

There were other Indians

hunting and fishing on Manhattan,

but Small Wolf wanted

to be alone.

So he pulled his canoe

up on the bank

and hid it,

and went into the forest.

When it got dark,

Small Wolf made camp.

He made a shelter,

and he made a fire.

He cooked a small bird he had shot.

And then he lay down.

But he did not go to sleep,

because the night was full of things.

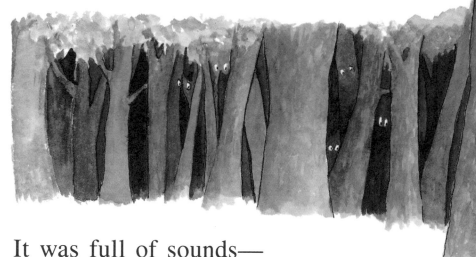

It was full of sounds—

WOO HOO! *Greeeeeeek! Owwwwwwww!*

Snap! Crackle! Pop!

GRK-*k-k-k-k*! Grotch!

BliggerbliggerbliggerYOW!

And it was full of eyes.

Small Wolf did not fall asleep

until daylight.

When he woke up,

he saw a path through the woods.

"I think I'll follow this

and see where it goes," he said.

"It may take me

to where there is good game."

So he said "Ya-hoo!"

a couple of times for good luck

and set off, ready for anything.

But he was not ready

for what happened next.

He came out of the woods,

and he could not believe what he saw.

21

He saw things

he had never seen before—

houses with chimneys,

and ships with sails,

and a house

with four arms that twirled around,

and a man whose face was all WHITE!

The man had a fat jaw

and cracks between his teeth.

Small Wolf thought

the man was wearing

some devil mask.

25

Off a ship

came odd animals.

26

There came horses

with long manes and tails.

There came cows

with short horns and black spots.

There came sheep

with curled horns and black faces.

There came pigs

with curled tails and stubby noses.

And they were so big and strange,

and made such queer sounds:

WHNNNNNNNY! MOO! BAAAAAAA!

and OINK!

Small Wolf was afraid.

"I did not come to hunt

this kind of thing," he said.

"They are too much for me!"

And he ran back into the woods.

He ran all the way back up the path

until he found his canoe,

and he paddled away from Manhattan

as fast as he could.

When Small Wolf got home,

he told his father

what he had seen.

"I saw a man

all painted white!" he said.

"His hands and face were white,

and his jaws were fat,

and he had teeth like a medicine man—

or a devil!"

"I know about the white men,"

said his father.

"They came some time ago.

They are all right,

if you leave them alone."

31

"But then there were animals!"

said Small Wolf.

"You never saw such animals!

Some have horns like this,

and some have horns like that,

and some have bushy tails,

and some have curly tails,

and they make noises

like WHNNNNNNY! MOO!

BAAA! and OINK!—

you would not believe it

unless you saw it!"

"All right," said his father.

"That sounds interesting.

I'll go and see."

"Interesting?" said Small Wolf.

"It's terrifying! Just wait!"

So they took the canoe

and went back to Manhattan.

34

"There!" said Small Wolf

when they reached the town.

"There are the animals!

Did you ever see anything like them?"

"They are odd," his father agreed.

"Let's ask someone

and see what we can find out."

So they went to a white man,

who looked startled to see them.

He raised his gun

and held it ready.

"What are those animals for?"

Small Wolf's father asked.

"They are for the farms,"

said the white man.

"And you'd better get along.

This land is ours now.

We paid for it."

"How can you pay for land?"

asked his father.

"Can you pay for the sky

or the sea?

Whom did you pay for the land?"

"We paid the Indians

who were here,"

the white man said.

"They were fishing in the pond.

Now, get going or I'll shoot."

He pointed his gun,

and cocked it with a small CLICK.

"You don't have to be afraid,"

said Small Wolf's father.

"We were only asking."

"I said get going,"

said the white man.

So Small Wolf and his father left.

"What Indians did he pay?"

Small Wolf asked

as they paddled away.

"The Canarsees," said his father,

"and they did not even live there.

They had no right to sell the land.

The land and the sky and the sea

are all Mother Earth

for everyone to use."

But the white men

did not see it that way.

They put up more houses

and spread out up the island.

Their animals went everywhere,

and ate the crops

the Indians had planted,

and trampled on the Indians' fields.

Finally

there were more white men

and their animals

than Indians.

The animals

that the Indians had hunted

were gone.

The Indians had a hard time

growing any crops,

and they were hungry.

One day Small Wolf's father

made a decision.

"I shall go and see

the leader of the white men," he said.

"I shall tell him

he is spoiling the land,

and I shall ask him

please to stop.

There is no reason

to destroy the land like this."

"May I come too?" Small Wolf asked.

"Yes," said his father.

"It is for your good I am asking."

So they set off

to find the leader of the white men.

Before they had gone very far,

they heard shouts

and saw men running,

and then there was a BANG!

and something went THUNK!

into a tree behind Small Wolf.

In the distance

they heard men shouting,

"Indians! Indians!"

"Hey!" said Small Wolf.

"What is this all about?"

"I don't know," his father said.

"Stand still and listen."

They listened,

and they heard more shouts.

Then came another BANG!

and a piece of bark

flew off a tree nearby.

"They're shooting at us!"

Small Wolf cried.

He ducked behind a tree,

and his father did the same.

"It looks that way,"

his father agreed.

"But that makes no sense."

He raised a hand to his mouth

and called,

"We want to talk!

Will your leader come

and talk with us?"

"Get out of here, you Indians!"

a voice shouted from the woods.

"Get back where you belong!"

And a third shot rang out,

and a bullet snarled

past Small Wolf's ear.

"I guess," his father said,

"they don't want to talk.

We might as well go back."

They went back,

and the next day his father

made another decision.

"There is plenty of land for all," he said.

"If we can't live here,

then we will just go

farther up the river.

If we go far enough,

they will never reach us."

So they packed their goods

and started off

to find a place

where the white men would not come.

They found a place

and settled down.

58

Then one day,

when Small Wolf was hunting,

he thought he saw a deer.

He got closer

and aimed his arrow.

Then he saw

it was not a deer.

It was a cow!

He went home

and told his father.

"That means they are here,"

his father said.

"We might as well move now,
before there is any trouble."

So off they went again.

And again.

And again.

And

again.

Author's Note

Although this fictional story is about Manhattan, Small Wolf and his father could be any of the American Indians who were displaced from their homes and hunting grounds by the white men. The Canarsee Indians, who "sold" Manhattan to the Dutch, had no more right to the land than anyone else—they lived in the Brooklyn area—and to them the idea of owning land made no more sense than owning the sky or the sea. They were happy to take the money the Dutch offered, and it wasn't until too late that they realized the white men's ideas about property were different from their own. This story was repeated, time after dismal time, until the Indians had nothing left.   —N.B.